HAWKS OF OUTREMER

BY

ROBERT E. HOWARD

British Library Cataloguing-in-Publication Data
A catalogue record for this book is available from the
British Library

Contents

Robert E. Howard

Robert Ervin Howard was born in Peaster, Texas in 1906. During his youth, his family moved between a variety of Texan boomtowns, and Howard – a bookish and somewhat introverted child – was steeped in the violent myths and legends of the Old South. Although he loved reading and learning, Howard developed a distinctly Texan, hardboiled outlook on the world. He became a passionate fan of boxing, taking it up at an amateur level, and from the age of nine began to write adventure tales of semi-historical bloodshed. In 1919, when Howard was thirteen, his family moved to the Central Texas hamlet of Cross Plains, where he would stay for the rest of his life.

At fifteen Howard began to read the pulp magazines of the day, and to write more seriously. The December 1922 issue of his high school newspaper featured two of his stories, 'Golden Hope Christmas' and 'West is West'. In 1924 he sold his first piece – a short caveman tale titled 'Spear and Fang' – for $16 to the not-yet-famous *Weird Tales* magazine. He published with the magazine regularly over the next few years. 1929 was a breakout year for Howard, in that the 23-year-old writer began to sell to other magazines, such as *Ghost Stories* and *Argosy,* both of whom had previously sent him hundreds of rejection slips. In 1930, he began a

1

correspondence with weird fiction master H. P. Lovecraft which ran up to his death six years later, and is regarded as one of the great correspondence cycles in all of fantasy literature.

It was partly due to Lovecraft's encouragement that Howard created his most famous character, Conan the Cimmerian. Conan – a barbarian-turned-King during the Hyborian Age, a mythical period of some 12,000 years ago – featured in seventeen *Weird Tales* stories between 1933 and 1936, and is now regarded as having spawned the 'sword and sorcery' genre, making Howard's influence on fantasy literature comparable to that of J. R. R. Tolkien's. The Conan stories have since been adapted many times, most famously in the series of films starring Arnold Schwarzenegger.

Howard was enjoying an all-time high in sales by the beginning of 1936, but he was also deeply upset by the ill health of his mother, who had fallen into a coma. On the morning of June 11, 1936, he asked an attending nurse whether she would ever recover, and the nurse replied negatively. Howard walked to his car, parked outside the family home in Cross Plains, and shot himself. He died eight hours later, aged just thirty.

"The still, white, creeping road slips on.
Marked by the bones of man and beast.
What comeliness and might have gone
    To pad the highway of the East!
    Long dynasties of fallen rose.
    The glories of a thousand wars.
    A million lovers' hearts compose
    The dust upon the road to Fars."

— Vansittart

CHAPTER I:
A MAN RETURNS

"Halt!" The bearded man-at-arms swung his pike about, growling like a surly mastiff. It paid to be wary on the road to Antioch. The stars blinked redly through the thick night and their light was not sufficient for the fellow to make out what sort of man it was who loomed so gigantically before him.

An iron-clad hand shot out suddenly and closed on the soldier's mailed shoulder in a grasp that numbed his whole arm. From beneath the helmet the guardsman saw the blaze of ferocious blue eyes that seemed lambent, even in the dark.

"Saints preserve us!" gasped the frightened man-at-arms, "Cormac FitzGeoffrey! Avaunt! Back to Hell with ye, like a good knight! I swear to you, sir--"

"Swear me no oaths," growled the knight. "What is this talk?"

"Are you not an incorporeal spirit?" mouthed the soldier. "Were you not slain by the Moorish corsairs on your homeward voyage?"

"By the accursed gods!" snarled FitzGeoffrey. "Does this hand feel like smoke?"

He sank his mailed fingers into the soldier's arm and grinned bleakly at the resultant howl.

"Enough of such mummery; tell me who is within that tavern."

"Only my master, Sir Rupert de Vaile, of Rouen."

"Good enough," grunted the other. "He is one of the few men I count friends, in the East or elsewhere."

The big warrior strode to the tavern door and entered, treading lightly as a cat despite his heavy armor. The man-at-arms rubbed his arm and stared after him curiously, noting, in the dim light, that FitzGeoffrey bore a shield with the horrific emblem of his family--a white grinning skull. The guardsman knew him of old--a turbulent character, a savage fighter and the only man among the Crusaders who had been esteemed stronger than Richard the Lion-hearted. But FitzGeoffrey had taken ship for his native isle even before Richard had departed from the Holy Land. The Third Crusade had ended in failure and disgrace; most of the Frankish knights had followed their kings homeward. What was this grim Irish killer doing on the road to Antioch?

Sir Rupert de Vaile, once of Rouen, now a lord of the fast-fading Outremer, turned as the great form bulked in the doorway. Cormac FitzGeoffrey was a fraction of an inch above six feet, but with his mighty shoulders and two hundred pounds of iron muscle, he seemed shorter. The

Norman stared in surprized recognition, and sprang to his feet. His fine face shone with sincere pleasure.

"Cormac, by the saints! Why, man, we heard that you were dead!"

Cormac returned the hearty grip, while his thin lips curved slightly in what would have been, in another man, a broad grin of greeting. Sir Rupert was a tall man, and well knit, but he seemed almost slight beside the huge Irish warrior who combined bulk with a sort of dynamic aggressiveness that was apparent in his every movement.

FitzGeoffrey was clean-shaven and the various scars that showed on his dark, grim face lent his already formidable features a truly sinister aspect. When he took off his plain visorless helmet and thrust back his mail coif, his square-cut, black hair that topped his low broad forehead contrasted strongly with his cold blue eyes. A true son of the most indomitable and savage race that ever trod the bloodstained fields of battle, Cormac FitzGeoffrey looked to be what he was--a ruthless fighter, born to the game of war, to whom the ways of violence and bloodshed were as natural as the ways of peace are to the average man.

Son of a woman the O'Briens and a renegade Norman knight, Geoffrey the Bastard, in whose veins, it is said, coursed the blood of William the Conqueror, Cormac had seldom known an hour of peace or ease in all his thirty years of violent life. He was born in a feud-torn and blood-drenched land, and raised in a heritage of hate and savagery. The ancient culture of Erin had long crumbled before the repeated onslaughts of Norsemen and Danes. Harried on all sides by cruel foes, the rising civilization of the Celts had faded before the fierce necessity of incessant conflict, and the merciless struggle for survival had made the Gaels as savage as the heathens who assailed them.

Now, in Cormac's time, war upon red war swept the crimson isle, where clan fought clan, and the Norman adventurers tore at one another's throats, or resisted the attacks of the Irish, playing tribe against tribe, while from Norway and the Orkneys the still half-pagan Vikings ravaged all impartially.

A vague realization of all this flashed through Sir Rupert's mind as he stood staring at his friend.

"We heard you were slain in a sea-fight off Sicily," he repeated.

Cormac shrugged his shoulders. "Many died then, it is true, and I was struck senseless by a stone from a ballista. Doubtless that is how the rumor started. But you see me, as much alive as ever."

"Sit down, old friend." Sir Rupert thrust forward one of the rude benches which formed part of the tavern's furniture. "What is forward in the West?"

Cormac took the wine goblet proffered him by a dark-skinned servitor, and drank deeply.

"Little of note," said he. "In France the king counts his pence and squabbles with his nobles. Richard--if he lives--languishes somewhere in Germany, 'tis thought. In England Shane--that is to say, John--oppresses the people and betrays the barons. And in Ireland--Hell!" He laughed shortly and without mirth. "What shall I say of Ireland but the same old tale? Gael and foreigner cut each other's throat and plot together against the king. John De Coursey, since Hugh de Lacy supplanted him as governor, has raged like a madman, burning and pillaging, while Donal O'Brien lurks in the west to destroy what remains. Yet, by Satan, I think this land is but little better."

"Yet there is peace of a sort now," murmured Sir Rupert.

"Aye--peace while the jackal Saladin gathers his powers," grunted Cormac. "Think you he will rest idle while Acre, Antioch and Tripoli remain in Christian hands? He but waits an excuse to seize the remnants of Outremer."

Sir Rupert shook his head, his eyes shadowed.

"It is a naked land and a bloody one. Were it not akin to blasphemy I could curse the day I followed my King eastward. Betimes I dream of the orchards of Normandy, the deep cool forests and the dreaming vineyards. Methinks my happiest hours were when a page of twelve years--"

"At twelve," grunted FitzGeoffrey, "I was running wild with shock-head kerns on the naked fens--I wore wolf skins, weighed near to fourteen stone, and had killed three men."

Sir Rupert looked curiously at his friend. Separated from Cormac's native land by a width of sea and the breadth of Britain, the Norman knew but little of the affairs in that far isle. But he knew vaguely that Cormac's life had not been an easy one. Hated by the Irish and despised by the Normans, he had paid back contempt and ill-treatment with savage hate and ruthless vengeance. It was known that he owned a shadow of allegiance only to the great house of Fitzgerald, who, as much Welsh as Norman, had even then begun to take up Irish customs and Irish quarrels.

"You wear another sword than that you wore when I saw you last."

"They break in my hands," said Cormac. "Three Turkish sabers went into the forging of the sword I wielded at Joppa--yet it shattered like glass in that sea-fight off Sicily. I took this from the body of a Norse sea-king who led a raid into Munster. It was forged in Norway--see the pagan runes on the steel?"

He drew the sword and the great blade shimmered bluely, like a thing alive in the candle light. The servants crossed themselves and Sir Rupert shook his head.

"You should not have drawn it here--they say blood follows such a sword."

"Bloodshed follows my trail anyway," growled Cormac. "This blade has already drunk FitzGeoffrey blood--with this that Norse sea-king slew my brother, Shane."

"And you wear such a sword?" exclaimed Sir Rupert in horror. "No good will come of that evil blade, Cormac!"

"Why not?" asked the big warrior impatiently. "It's a good blade--I wiped out the stain of my brother's blood when I slew his slayer. By Satan, but that sea-king was a grand sight in his coat of mail with silvered scales. His silvered helmet was strong too--ax, helmet and skull shattered together."

"You had another brother, did you not?"

"Aye--Donal. Eochaidh O'Donnell ate his heart out after the battle at Coolmanagh. There was a feud between us at the time, so it may be Eochaidh merely saved me the trouble--but for all that I burned the O'Donnell in his own castle."

"How came you to first ride on the Crusade?" asked Sir Rupert curiously. "Were you stirred with a desire to cleanse your soul by smiting the Paynim?"

"Ireland was too hot for me," answered the Norman-Gael candidly. "Lord Shamus MacGearailt--James Fitzgerald--wished to make peace with the English king and I feared he would buy favor by delivering me into the hands of the king's governor. As there was feud between my family and most of the Irish clans, there was nowhere for me to go. I was about to seek my fortune in Scotland when young

Eamonn Fitzgerald was stung by the hornet of Crusade and I accompanied him."

"But you gained favor with Richard--tell me the tale."

"Soon told. It was on the plains of Azotus when we came to grips with the Turks. Aye, you were there! I was fighting alone in the thick of the fray and helmets and turbans were cracking like eggs all around when I noted a strong knight in the forefront of our battle. He cut deeper and deeper into the close-ranked lines of the heathen and his heavy mace scattered brains like water. But so dented was his shield and so stained with blood his armor, I could not tell who he might be.

"But suddenly his horse went down and in an instant he was hemmed in on all sides by the howling fiends who bore him down by sheer weight of numbers. So hacking a way to his side I dismounted--"

"Dismounted?" exclaimed Sir Rupert in amazement.

Cormac's head jerked up in irritation at the interruption. "Why not?" he snapped. "I am no French she-knight to fear wading in the muck--anyway, I fight better on foot. Well, I cleared a space with a sweep or so of my sword, and the fallen knight, the press being lightened, came up roaring like a bull and swinging his blood-clotted mace with such fury he nearly brained me as well as the Turks. A charge of English knights swept the heathen away and when he lifted his visor I saw I had succored Richard of England.

"'Who are you and who is your master?' said he.

"'I am Cormac FitzGeoffrey and I have no master,' said I. 'I followed young Eamonn Fitzgerald to the Holy Land and since he fell before the walls of Acre, I seek my fortune alone.'

"'What think ye of me as a master?' asked he, while the battle raged half a bow-shot about us.

"'You fight reasonably well for a man with Saxon blood in his veins,' I answered, 'but I own allegiance to no English king.'

"He swore like a trooper. 'By the bones of the saints,' said he, 'that had cost another man his head. You saved my life, but for this insolence, no prince shall knight you!'

"'Keep your knighthoods and be damned,' said I. 'I am a chief in Ireland--but we waste words; yonder are pagan heads to be smashed.'

"Later he bade me to his royal presence and waxed merry with me; a rare drinker he is, though a fool withal. But I distrust kings--I attached myself to the train of a brave and gallant young knight of France--the Sieur Gerard de Gissclin, full of insane ideals of chivalry, but a noble youth.

"When peace was made between the hosts, I heard hints of a renewal of strife between the Fitzgeralds and the Le Boteliers, and Lord Shamus having been slain by Nial Mac Art, and I being in favor with the king anyway, I took leave of Sieur Gerard and betook myself back to Erin.

Well--we swept Ormond with torch and sword and hanged old Sir William le Botelier to his own barbican. Then, the Geraldines having no particular need of my sword at the moment, I bethought myself once more of Sieur Gerard, to whom I owed my life and which debt I have not yet had opportunity to pay. How, Sir Rupert, dwells he still in his castle of Ali-El-Yar?"

Sir Rupert's face went suddenly white, and he leaned back as if shrinking from something. Cormac's head jerked up and his dark face grew more forbidding and fraught with somber potentialities. He seized the Norman's arm in an unconsciously savage grip.

"Speak, man," he rasped. "What ails you?"

"Sieur Gerard," half-whispered Sir Rupert. "Had you not heard? Ali-El-Yar lies in smoldering ruins and Gerard is dead."

Cormac snarled like a mad dog, his terrible eyes blazing with a fearful light. He shook Sir Rupert in the intensity of his passion.

"Who did the deed? He shall die, were he Emperor of Byzantium!"

"I know not!" Sir Rupert gasped, his mind half-stunned by the blast of the Gael's primitive fury. "There be foul rumors--Sieur Gerard loved a girl in a sheik's harem, it is said. A horde of wild riders from the desert assailed his castle and a rider broke through to ask aid of the baron Conrad Von Gonler. But Conrad refused--"

"Aye!" snarled Cormac, with a savage gesture. "He hated Gerard because long ago the youngster had the best of him at sword-play on shipboard before old Frederick Barbarossa's eyes. And what then?"

"Ali-El-Yar fell with all its people. Their stripped and mutilated bodies lay among the coals, but no sign was found of Gerard. Whether he died before or after the attack on the castle is not known, but dead he must be, since no demand for ransom has been made."

"Thus Saladin keeps the peace!"

Sir Rupert, who knew Cormac's unreasoning hatred for the great Kurdish sultan, shook his head. "This was no work of his--there is incessant bickering along the border--Christian as much at fault as Moslem. It could not be otherwise with Frankish barons holding castles in the very heart of Muhammadan country. There are many private feuds and there are wild desert and mountain tribes who owe no lordship even to Saladin, and wage their own wars. Many suppose that the sheik Nureddin El Ghor destroyed Ali-El-Yar and put Sieur Gerard to death."

Cormac caught up his helmet.

"Wait!" exclaimed Sir Rupert, rising. "What would you do?"

Cormac laughed savagely. "What would I do? I have eaten the bread of the de Gissclins. Am I a jackal to sneak home and leave my patron to the kites? Out on it!"

"But wait," Sir Rupert urged. "What will your life be worth if you ride on Nureddin's trail alone? I will return to Antioch and gather my retainers; we will avenge your friend together."

"Nureddin is a half-independent chief and I am a masterless wanderer," rumbled the Norman-Gael, "but you are Seneschal of Antioch. If you ride over the border with your men-at-arms, the swine Saladin will take advantage to break the truce and sweep the remnants of the Christian kingdoms into the sea. They are but weak shells, as it is, shadows of the glories of Baldwin and Bohemund. No--the FitzGeoffreys wreak their own vengeance. I ride alone."

He jammed his helmet into place and with a gruff "Farewell!" he turned and strode into the night, roaring for his horse. A trembling servant brought the great black stallion, which reared and snorted with a flash of wicked teeth. Cormac seized the reins and savagely jerked down the rearing steed, swinging into the saddle before the pawing front hoofs touched earth.

"Hate and the glutting of vengeance!" he yelled savagely, as the great stallion whirled away, and Sir Rupert, staring bewilderedly after him, heard the swiftly receding clash of the brazen-shod hoofs. Cormac FitzGeoffrey was riding east.

CHAPTER II:
THE CAST OF AN AX

White dawn surged out of the Orient to break in rose-red billows on the hills of Outremer. The rich tints softened the rugged outlines, deepened the blue wastes of the sleeping desert.

The castle of the baron Conrad Von Gonler frowned out over a wild and savage waste. Once a stronghold of the Seljuk Turks, its metamorphosis into the manor of a Frankish lord had abated none of the Eastern menace of its appearance. The walls had been strengthened and a barbican built in place of the usual wide gates. Otherwise the keep had not been altered.

Now in the dawn a grim, dark figure rode up to the deep, waterless moat which encircled the stronghold, and smote with iron-clad fist on hollow-ringing shield until the echoes reverberated among the hills. A sleepy man-at-arms thrust his head and his pike over the wall above the barbican and bellowed a challenge.

The lone rider threw back his helmeted head, disclosing a face dark with a passion that an all-night's ride had not cooled in the least.

"You keep rare watch here," roared Cormac FitzGeoffrey. "Is it because you're so hand-in-glove with the Paynim that you fear no attack? Where is that ale-guzzling swine you call your liege?"

"The baron is at wine," the fellow answered sullenly, in broken English.

"So early?" marveled Cormac.

"Nay," the other gave a surly grin, "he has feasted all night."

"Wine-bibber! Glutton!" raged Cormac. "Tell him I have business with him."

"And what shall I say your business is, Lord FitzGeoffrey?" asked the carl, impressed.

"Tell him I bring a passport to Hell!" yelled Cormac, gnashing his teeth, and the scared soldier vanished like a puppet on a string.

The Norman-Gael sat his horse impatiently, shield slung on his shoulders, lance in its stirrup socket, and to his surprise, suddenly the barbican door swung wide and out of it strutted a fantastic figure. Baron Conrad Von Gonler was short and fat; broad of shoulder and portly of belly, though still a young man. His long arms and wide shoulders had gained him a reputation as a deadly broadsword man, but just now he looked little of the fighter. Germany and Austria sent many noble knights to the Holy Land. Baron Von Gonler was not one of them.

His only arm was a gold-chased dagger in a richly brocaded sheath. He wore no armor, and his costume, flaming with gay silk and heavy with gold, was a bizarre mingling of European gauds and Oriental finery. In one hand, on each finger of which sparkled a great jewel, he held a golden wine goblet. A band of drunken revelers reeled out behind him--minnesingers, dwarfs, dancing girls, wine-companions, vacuous-faced, blinking like owls in the daylight. All the boot-kissers and hangers-on that swarm after a rich and degenerate lord trooped with their master--scum of both races. The luxury of the East had worked quick ruin on Baron Von Gonler.

"Well," shouted the baron, "who is it wishes to interrupt my drinking?"

"Any but a drunkard would know Cormac FitzGeoffrey," snarled the horseman, his lip writhing back from his strong teeth in contempt. "We have an account to settle."

That name and Cormac's tone had been enough to sober any drunken knight of the Outremer. But Von Gonler was not only drunk; he was a degenerate fool. The baron took a long drink while his drunken crew stared curiously at the savage figure on the other side of the dry moat, whispering to one another.

"Once you were a man, Von Gonler," said Cormac in a tone of concentrated venom; "now you have become a groveling debauchee. Well, that's your own affair. The matter I have in mind is another--why did you refuse aid to the Sieur de Gissclin?"

The German's puffy, arrogant face took on new hauteur.
He pursed his thick lips haughtily, while his bleared eyes
blinked over his bulbous nose like an owl. He was an image
of pompous stupidity that made Cormac grind his teeth.

"What was the Frenchman to me?" the baron retorted
brutally. "It was his own fault--out of a thousand girls he
might have taken, the young fool tried to steal one a sheik
wanted himself. He, the purity of honor! Bah!"

He added a coarse jest and the creatures with him
screamed with mirth, leaping and flinging themselves into
obscene postures. Cormac's sudden and lion-like roar of fury
gave them pause.

"Conrad Von Gonler!" thundered the maddened Gael,
"I name you liar, traitor and coward--dastard, poltroon and
villain! Arm yourself and ride out here on the plain. And
haste--I can not waste much time on you--I must kill you
quick and ride on lest another vermin escape me."

The baron laughed cynically, "Why should I fight you?
You are not even a knight. You wear no knightly emblem on
your shield."

"Evasions of a coward," raged FitzGeoffrey. "I am a chief
in Ireland and I have cleft the skulls of men whose boots you
are not worthy to touch. Will you arm yourself and ride out,
or are you become the swinish coward I deem you?"

Von Gonler laughed in scornful anger.

"I need not risk my hide fighting you. I will not fight you, but I will have my men-at-arms fill your hide with crossbow bolts if you tarry longer."

"Von Gonler," Cormac's voice was deep and terrible in its brooding menace, "will you fight, or die in cold blood?"

The German burst into a sudden brainless shout of laughter.

"Listen to him!" he roared. "He threatens me--he on the other side of the moat, with the drawbridge lifted--I here in the midst of my henchmen!"

He smote his fat thigh and roared with his fool's laughter, while the debased men and women who served his pleasures laughed with him and insulted the grim Irish warrior with shrill anathema and indecent gestures. And suddenly Cormac, with a bitter curse, rose in his stirrups, snatched his battle-ax from his saddle-bow and hurled it with all his mighty strength.

The men-at-arms on the towers cried out and the dancing girls screamed. Von Gonler had thought himself to be out of reach--but there is no such thing as being out of reach of Norman-Irish vengeance. The heavy ax hissed as it clove the air and dashed out Baron Conrad's brains.

The fat, gross body buckled to the earth like a mass of melted tallow, one fat, white hand still gripping the empty wine goblet. The gay silks and cloth-of-gold were dabbled in a deeper red than ever was sold in the bazaar, and the jesters and dancers scattered like birds, screaming at the sight of that blasted head and the crimson ruin that had been a human face.

Cormac FitzGeoffrey made a fierce, triumphant gesture and voiced a deep-chested yell of such ferocious exultation that men blenched to hear. Then wheeling his black steed suddenly, he raced away before the dazed soldiers could get their wits together to send a shower of arrows after him.

He did not gallop far. The great steed was weary from a hard night's travel. Cormac soon swung in behind a jutting crag, and reining his horse up a steep incline, halted and looked back the way he had come. He was out of sight of the keep, but he heard no sounds of pursuit. A wait of some half-hour convinced him that no attempt had been made to follow him. It was dangerous and foolhardy to ride out of a safe castle into these hills. Cormac might well have been one of an ambushing force.

At any rate, whatever his enemies' thoughts were on the subject, it was evident that he need expect no present attempt at retaliation, and he grunted with angry satisfaction. He never shunned a fight, but just now he had other business on hand.

Cormac rode eastward.

CHAPTER III:
THE ROAD TO EL GHOR

The way to El Ghor was rough indeed. Cormac wound his way between huge jagged boulders, across deep ravines and up treacherous steeps. The sun slowly climbed toward the zenith and the heat waves began to dance and shimmer. The sun beat fiercely on Cormac's helmeted head, and glancing back from the bare rocks, dazzled his narrowed eyes. But the big warrior gave no heed; in his own land he learned to defy sleet and snow and bitter cold; following the standard of Coeur de Lion, before the shimmering walls of Acre, on the dusty plains of Azotus, and before Joppa, he had become inured to the blaze of the Oriental sun, to the glare of naked sands, to the slashing dust winds.

At noon he halted long enough to allow the black stallion an hour's rest in the shade of a giant boulder. A tiny spring bubbled there, known to him of old, and it slaked the thirst of the man and the horse. The stallion cropped eagerly at the scrawny fringe of grass about the spring and Cormac ate of the dried meats he carried in a small pouch. Here he had watered his steed in the old days, when he rode with Gerard. Ali-El-Yar lay to the west; in the night he had swung around it in a wide circle as he rode to the castle of Von Gonler. He had had no wish to gaze on the moldering ruins.

The nearest Moslem chief of any importance was Nureddin El Ghor, who with his brother-at-arms, Kosru Malik, the Seljuk, held the castle of El Ghor, in the hills to the east.

Cormac rode on stolidly through the savage heat. As mid-afternoon neared he rode up out of a deep, wide defile and came onto the higher levels of the hills. Up this defile he had ridden aforetime to raid the wild tribes to the east, and on the small plateaus at the head of the defile stood a gibbet where Sieur Gerard de Gissclin had once hanged a red-handed Turkoman chief as a warning to those tribes.

Now, as FitzGeoffrey rode up on the plateau, he saw the old tree again bore fruit. His keen eyes made out a human form suspended in midair, apparently by the wrists. A tall warrior in the peaked helmet and light mail shirt of a Moslem stood beneath, tentatively prodding at the victim with a spear, making the body sway and spin on the rope. A bay Turkoman horse stood near. Cormac's cold eyes narrowed. The man on the rope--his naked body glistened too white in the sun for a Turk. The Norman-Gael touched spurs to the black stallion and swept across the plateau at a headlong run.

At the sudden thunder of hoofs the Muhammadan started and whirled. Dropping the spear with which he had been tormenting the captive, he mounted swiftly, stringing a short heavy bow as he did so. This done, and his left forearm thrust through the straps of a small round buckler, he trotted out to meet the onset of the Frank.

Cormac was approaching at a thundering charge, eyes glaring over the edge of his grim shield. He knew that this Turk would never meet him as a Frankish knight would have met him--breast to breast. The Moslem would avoid his ponderous rushes, and circling him on his nimbler steed, drive in shaft after shaft until one found its mark. But he rushed on as recklessly as if he had never before encountered Saracen tactics.

Now the Turk bent his bow and the arrow glanced from Cormac's shield. They were barely within javelin cast of each other, but even as the Moslem laid another shaft to string, doom smote him. Cormac, without checking his headlong gait, suddenly rose in his stirrups and gripping his long lance in the middle, cast it like a javelin. The unexpectedness of the move caught the Seljuk off guard and he made the mistake of throwing up his shield instead of dodging. The lance-head tore through the light buckler and crashed full on his mail-clad breast. The point bent on his hauberk without piercing the links, but the terrific impact dashed the Turk from his saddle and as he rose, dazed and groping for his scimitar, the great black stallion was already looming horrific over him, and under those frenzied hoofs he went down, torn and shattered.

Without a second glance at his victim Cormac rode under the gibbet and rising in the saddle, stared into the face of he who swung therefrom.

"By Satan," muttered the big warrior, "'tis Micaul na Blaos--Michael de Blois, one of Gerard's squires. What devil's work is this?"

Drawing his sword he cut the rope and the youth slid into his arms. Young Michael's lips were parched and swollen, his eyes dull with suffering. He was naked except for short leathern breeks, and the sun had dealt cruelly with his fair skin. Blood from a slight scalp wound caked his yellow hair, and there were shallow cuts on his limbs--marks left by his tormentor's spear.

Cormac laid the young Frenchman in the shade cast by the motionless stallion and trickled water through the parched lips from his canteen. As soon as he could speak, Michael croaked: "Now I know in truth that I am dead, for there is but one knight ever rode in Outremer who could cast a long lance like a javelin--and Cormac FitzGeoffrey has been dead for many months. But I be dead, where is Gerard--and Yulala?"

"Rest and be at ease," growled Cormac. "You live--and so do I."

He loosed the cords that had cut deep into the flesh of Michael's wrists and set himself to gently rub and massage the numb arms. Slowly the delirium faded from the youth's eyes. Like Cormac, he too came of a race that was tough as spring steel; an hour's rest and plenty of water, and his intense vitality asserted itself.

"How long have you hung from this gibbet?" asked Cormac.

"Since dawn." Michael's eyes were grim as he rubbed his lacerated wrists. "Nureddin and Kosru Malik said that since Sieur Gerard once hanged one of their race here, it was fitting that one of Gerard's men should grace this gibbet."

"Tell me how Gerard died," growled the Irish warrior. "Men hint at foul tales--"

Michael's fine eyes filled with tears. "Ah, Cormac, I who loved him, brought about his death. Listen--there is more to this than meets the casual eye. I think that Nureddin and his comrade-at-arms have been stung by the hornet of empire. It is in my mind that they, with various dog-knights among the Franks, dream of a mongrel kingdom among these hills, which shall hold allegiance neither to Saladin nor any king of the West.

"They begin to broaden their holdings by treachery. The nearest Christian hold was that of Ali-El-Yar, of course. Sieur Gerard was a true knight, peace be upon his fair soul, and he must be removed. All this I learned later--would to God I had known it beforehand! Among Nureddin's slaves is a Persian girl named Yulala, and with this innocent tool of their evil wishes, the twain sought to ensnare my lord--

to slay at once his body and his good name. And God help me, through me they succeeded where otherwise they had failed.

"For my lord Gerard was honorable beyond all men. When in peace, and at Nureddin's invitation, he visited El Ghor, he paid no heed to Yulala's blandishments. For according to the commands of her masters, which she dared not disobey, the girl allowed Gerard to look on her, unveiled, as if by chance, and she pretended affection for him. But Gerard gave her no heed. But I--I fell victim to her charms."

Cormac snorted in disgust. Michael clutched his arm.

"Cormac," he cried, "bethink you--all men are not iron like you! I swear I loved Yulala from the moment I first set eyes on her--and she loved me! I contrived to see her again--to steal into El Ghor itself--"

"Whence men got the tale that it was Gerard who was carrying on an affair with Nureddin's slave," snarled FitzGeoffrey.

Michael hid his face in his hands. "Mine the fault," he groaned. "Then one night a mute brought a note signed by Yulala--apparently--begging me to come with Sieur Gerard and his men-at-arms and save her from a frightful fate--our love had been discovered, the note read, and they were about to torture her. I was wild with rage and fear. I went to Gerard and told him all, and he, white soul of honor, vowed to aid me. He could not break the truce and bring Saladin's wrath upon the Christian's cities, but he donned his mail and rode forth alone with me. We would see if there was any way whereby we might steal Yulala away, secretly; if not, my lord would go boldly to Nureddin and ask the girl as a gift, or offer to pay a great ransom for her. I would marry her.

"Well, when we reached the place outside the wall of El Ghor, where I was wont to meet Yulala, we found we were trapped. Nureddin, Kosru Malik and their warriors rose suddenly about us on all sides. Nureddin first spoke to Gerard, telling him of the trap he had set and baited, hoping to entice my lord into his power alone. And the Moslem laughed to think that the chance love of a squire had drawn Gerard into the trap where the carefully wrought plan had failed. As for the missive--Nureddin wrote that himself, believing, in his craftiness, that Sieur Gerard would do just as indeed he did.

"Nureddin and the Turk offered to allow Gerard to join them in their plan of empire. They told him plainly that his castle and lands were the price a certain powerful nobleman asked in return for his alliance, and they offered alliance with Gerard instead of this noble. Sieur Gerard merely answered that so long as life remained in him, he would keep faith with his king and his creed, and at the word the Moslems rolled on us like a wave.

"Ah, Cormac, Cormac, had you but been there with our men-at-arms! Gerard bore himself right manfully as was his wont--back to back we fought and I swear to you that we trod a knee-deep carpet of the dead before Gerard fell and they dragged me down. 'Christ and the Cross!' were his last words, as the Turkish spears and swords pierced him through and through. And his fair body--naked and gashed, and thrown to the kites and the jackals!"

Michael sobbed convulsively, beating his fists together in his agony. Cormac rumbled deep in his chest like a savage bull. Blue lights burned and flickered in his eyes.

"And you?" he asked harshly.

"Me they flung into a dungeon for torture," answered Michael, "but that night Yulala came to me. An old servitor who loved her, and who had dwelt in El Ghor before it fell to Nureddin, freed me and led us both through a secret passage that leads from the torture chamber, beyond the wall. We went into the hills on foot and without weapons and wandered there for days, hiding from the horsemen sent forth to hunt us down. Yesterday we were recaptured and brought back to El Ghor. An arrow had struck down the old slave who showed us the passageway, unknown to the present masters of the castle, and we refused to tell how we had escaped though Nureddin threatened us with torture. This dawn he brought me forth from the castle and hanged me to this gibbet, leaving that one to guard me. What he has done to Yulala, God alone knows."

"You knew that Ali-El-Yar had fallen?"

"Aye," Michael nodded dully. "Kosru Malik boasted of it. The lands of Gerard now fall heir to his enemy, the traitor knight who will come to Nureddin's aid when the Moslem strikes for a crown."

"And who is this traitor?" asked Cormac softly.

"The baron Conrad Von Gonler, whom I swear to spit like a hare--"

Cormac smiled thinly and bleakly. "Swear me no oaths. Von Gonler has been in Hell since dawn. I knew only that he refused to come to Gerard's aid. I could have slain him no deader had I known his whole infamy."

Michael's eyes blazed. "A de Gissclin to the rescue!" he shouted fiercely. "I thank thee, old war-dog! One traitor is accounted for--what now? Shall Nureddin and the Turk live while two men wear de Gissclin steel?"

"Not if steel cuts and blood runs red," snarled Cormac. "Tell me of this secret way--nay, waste no time in words-- show me this secret way. If you escaped thereby, why should we not enter the same way? Here--take the arms from that carrion while I catch his steed which I see browses on the moss among the rocks. Night is not far away; mayhap we can gain through to the interior of the castle--there--"

His big hands clenched into iron sledges and his terrible eyes blazed; in his whole bearing there was apparent a plain tale of fire and carnage, of spears piercing bosoms and swords splitting skulls.

CHAPTER IV:
THE FAITH OF CORMAC

When Cormac FitzGeoffrey took up the trail to El Ghor again, one would have thought at a glance that a Turk rode with him. Michael de Blois rode the bay Turkoman steed and wore the peaked Turkish helmet. He was girt with the curved scimitar and carried the bow and quiver of arrows, but he did not wear the mail shirt; the hammering hoofs of the plunging stallion had battered and brayed it out of all usefulness.

The companions took a circuitous route into the hills to avoid outposts, and it was dusk before they looked down on the towers of El Ghor which stood, grim and sullen, girt on three sides by scowling hills. Westward a broad road wound down the steeps on which the castle stood. On all other sides ravine-cut slopes straggled to the beetling walls. They had made such a wide circle that they now stood in the hills almost directly east of the keep, and Cormac, gazing westward over the turrets, spoke suddenly to his friend.

"Look--a cloud of dust far out on the plain--"

Michael shook his head: "Your eyes are far keener than mine. The hills are so clouded with the blue shadows of twilight I can scarcely make out the blurred expanse that is the plain beyond, much less discern any movement upon it."

"My life has often depended on my eyesight," growled the Norman-Gael. "Look closely--see that tongue of plainsland that cleaves far into the hills like a broad valley, to the north? A band of horsemen, riding hard, are just entering the defiles, if I may judge by the cloud of dust they raise. Doubtless a band of raiders returning to El Ghor. Well-- they are in the hills now where going is rough and it will be hours before they get to the castle. Let us to our task--stars are blinking in the east."

They tied their horses in a place hidden from sight of any watcher below down among the gullies. In the last dim light of dusk they saw the turbans of the sentries on the towers, but gliding among boulders and defiles, they kept well concealed. At last Michael turned into a deep ravine.

"This leads into the subterranean corridor," said he. "God grant it has not been discovered by Nureddin. He had his warriors searching for something of the sort, suspecting its existence when we refused to tell how we had escaped."

They passed along the ravine, which grew narrower and deeper, for some distance, feeling their way; then Michael halted with a groan. Cormac, groping forward, felt iron bars, and as his eyes grew accustomed to the darkness, made out an opening like the mouth of a cave. Solid iron sills had been firmly bolted into the solid rock, and into these sills were set heavy bars, too close together to allow the most slender human to slip through.

"They have found the tunnel and closed it," groaned Michael. "Cormac, what are we to do?"

Cormac came closer and laid hands tentatively on the bars. Night had fallen and it was so dark in the ravine even his catlike eyes could hardly make out objects close at hand. The big Norman-Celt took a deep breath, and gripping a bar in each mighty hand, braced his iron legs and slowly exerted all his incredible strength. Michael, watching in amazement, sensed rather than saw the great muscles roll and swell under the pliant mail, the veins swell in the giant's forehead and sweat burst out. The bars groaned and creaked, and even as Michael remembered that this man was stronger than King Richard himself, the breath burst from Cormac's lips in an explosive grunt and simultaneously the bars gave way like reeds in his iron hands. One came away, literally torn from its sockets, and the others bent deeply. Cormac gasped and shook the sweat out of his eyes, tossing the bar aside.

"By the saints," muttered Michael, "are you man or devil, Cormac FitzGeoffrey? That is a feat I deemed even beyond your power."

"Enough words," grunted the Norman. "Let us make haste, if we can squeeze through. It's likely that we'll find a guard in this tunnel, but it's a chance we must take. Draw your steel and follow me."

It was as dark as the maw of Hades in the tunnel. They groped their way forward, expecting every minute to blunder into a trap, and Michael, stealing close at the heels of his friend, cursed the pounding of his own heart and wondered at the ability of the giant to move stealthily and with no rattling of arms.

To the comrades it seemed that they groped forward in the darkness for an eternity, and just as Michael leaned forward to whisper that he believed they were inside the castle's outer walls, a faint glow was observed ahead. Stealing warily forward they came to a sharp turn in the corridor around which shone the light. Peering cautiously about the corner they saw that the light emanated from a flickering torch thrust into a niche in the wall, and beside this stood a tall Turk, yawning as he leaned on his spear. Two other Moslems lay sleeping on their cloaks nearby. Evidently Nureddin did not lay too much trust in the bars with which he had blocked the entrance.

"The guard," whispered Michael, and Cormac nodded, stepping back and drawing his companion with him. The Norman-Gael's wary eyes had made out a flight of stone steps beyond the warriors, with a heavy door at the top.

"These seem to be all the weapon-men in the tunnel," muttered Cormac. "Loose a shaft at the waking warrior--and do not miss."

Michael fitted notch to string, and leaning close to the angle of the turn, aimed at the Turk's throat, just above the hauberk. He silently cursed the flickering, illusive light. Suddenly the drowsy warrior's head jerked up and he glared in their direction, suspicion flaring his eyes. Simultaneously came the twang of the loosed string and the Turk staggered and went down, gurgling horribly and clawing at the shaft that transfixed his bull neck.

The other two, awakened by their comrade's death throes and the sudden swift drum of feet on the ground, started up--and were cut down as they rubbed at sleep-filled eyes and groped for weapons.

"That was well done," growled Cormac, shaking the red drops from his steel. "There was no sound that should have carried through yonder door. Still, if it be bolted from within, our work is useless and we undone."

But it was not bolted, as the presence of the warriors in the tunnel suggested. As Cormac gently opened the heavy iron door, a sudden pain-fraught whimper from the other side electrified them.

"Yulala!" gasped Michael, whitening. "'Tis the torture chamber, and that is her voice! In God's name, Cormac--in!"

And the big Norman-Gael recklessly flung the door wide and leaped through like a charging tiger, with Michael at his heels. They halted short. It was the torture chamber, right enough, and on the floor and the walls stood or hung all the hellish appliances that the mind of man has invented for the torment of his brother. Three people were in the dungeon and two of these were bestial-faced men in leathern breeches, who looked up, startled, as the Franks entered. The third was a girl who lay bound to a sort of bench, naked as the day she was born. Coals glowed in braziers nearby, and one of the mutes was in the very act of reaching for a pair of white-hot pinchers. He crouched now, glaring in amazement, his arm still outstretched.

From the white throat of the captive girl burst a piteous cry.

"Yulala!" Michael cried out fiercely and leaped forward, a red mist floating before his eyes. One of the beast-faced mutes was before him, lifting a short sword, but the young Frank, without checking his stride, brought down his scimitar in a sweeping arc that drove the curved blade through scalp and skull. Wrenching his weapon free, he dropped to his knees beside the torture bench, a great sob tearing his throat.

"Yulala! Yulala! Oh girl, what have they done to you?"

"Michael, my beloved!" Her great dark eyes were like stars in the mist. "I knew you would come. They have not tortured me--save for a whipping--they were just about to begin--"

The other mute had glided swiftly toward Cormac as a snake glides, knife in hand.

"Satan!" grunted the big warrior. "I won't sully my steel with such blood--"

His left hand shot out and caught the mute's wrist and there was a crunch of splintering bones. The knife flew from the mute's fingers, which spread wide suddenly like an inflated glove. Blood burst from the fingertips and the creature's mouth gaped in silent agony. And at that instant Cormac's right hand closed on his throat and through the open lips burst a red deluge of blood as the Norman's iron fingers ground flesh and vertebrae to a crimson pulp.

Flinging aside the sagging corpse, Cormac turned to Michael, who had freed the girl and now was nearly crushing her in his arms as he gripped her close in a very passion of relief and joy. A heavy hand on his shoulder brought him back to a realization of their position. Cormac had found a cloak and this he wrapped about the naked girl.

"Go, at once," he said swiftly. "It may not be long before others come to take the place of the guards in the tunnel. Here--you have no armor--take my shield--no, don't argue. You may need it to protect the girl from arrows if you--if we, are pursued. Haste now--"

"But you, Cormac?" Michael lingered, hesitant.

"I will make fast that outer door," said the Norman. "I can heap benches against it. Then I will follow you. But don't wait for me. This is a command, do you understand? Hasten through the tunnel and go to the horses. There, instantly mount the Turkoman horse and ride! I will follow by another route--aye, by a road none but I can ride! Ride ye to Sir Rupert de Vaile, Seneschal of Antioch. He is our friend; hasten now."

Cormac stood a moment in the doorway at the head of the stairs and watched Michael and the girl hurry down the steps, past the place where the silent sentries lay, and vanish about the turn in the tunnel. Then he turned back into the torture chamber and closed the door. He crossed the room, threw the bolt on the outer door and swung it wide. He gazed up a winding flight of stairs. Cormac's face was immobile. He had voluntarily sealed his doom.

The giant Norman-Celt was an opportunist. He knew that such chance as had led him into the heart of his foe's stronghold was not likely to favor him again. Life was uncertain in Outremer; if he waited for another opportunity to strike at Nureddin and Kosru Malik, that opportunity might not come. This was his best opportunity for the vengeance for which his barbaric soul lusted.

That he would lose his own life in the consummating of that vengeance made no difference. Men were born to die in battle, according to his creed, and Cormac FitzGeoffrey secretly leaned toward the belief of his Viking ancestors in a Valhalla for the souls loosed gloriously in the clash of swords. Michael, having found the girl, had instantly forgotten the original plan of vengeance. Cormac had no blame for him; life and love were sweet to the young. But the grim Irish warrior owed a debt to the murdered Gerard and was prepared to pay with his own life. Thus Cormac kept faith with the dead.

He wished that he could have bade Michael ride the black stallion, but he knew that the horse would allow none but himself to bestride it. Now it would fall into Moslem hands, he thought with a sigh. He went up the stairs.

CHAPTER V.
THE LION OF ISLAM

At the top of the stairs, Cormac came into a corridor and along this he strode swiftly but warily, the Norse sword shimmering bluely in his hand. Going at random he turned into another corridor and here came full on a Turkish warrior, who stopped short, agape, seeing a supernatural horror in this grim slayer who strode like a silent phantom of death through the castle. Before the Turk could regain his wits, the blue sword shore through his neck cords.

Cormac stood above his victim for a moment, listening intently. Somewhere ahead of him he heard a low hum of voices, and the attitude of this Turk, with shield and drawn scimitar, had suggested that he stood guard before some chamber door. An irregular torch faintly illumined the wide corridor, and Cormac, groping in the semidarkness for a door, found instead a wide portal masked by heavy silk curtains. Parting them cautiously he gazed through into a great room thronged with armed men.

Warriors in mail and peaked helmets, and bearing wide-pointed, curved swords, lined the walls, and on silken cushions sat the chieftains--rulers of El Ghor and their satellites. Across the room sat Nureddin El Ghor, tall, lean, with a high-bridged, thin nose and keen dark eyes; his whole aspect distinctly hawk-like. His Semitic features contrasted with the Turks about him. His lean strong hand continually caressed the ivory hilt of a long, lean saber, and he wore a shirt of mesh-mail. A renegade chief from southern Arabia, this sheik was a man of great ability; his dream of an independent kingdom in these hills was no mad hashish hallucination. Let him win the alliance of a few Seljuk chiefs, of a few Frankish renegades like Von Gonler, and with the hordes of Arabs, Turks and Kurds that would assuredly flock to his banner, Nureddin would be a menace both to Saladin and the Franks who still clung to the fringes of Outremer. Among the mailed Turks Cormac saw the sheepskin caps and wolf skins of wild chiefs from beyond the hills--Kurds and Turkomans. Already the Arab's fame was spreading, if such unstable warriors as these were rallying to him.

Near the curtain-hung doorway sat Kosru Malik, known to Cormac of old, a warrior typical of his race, strongly built, of medium height, with a dark cruel face. Even as he sat in council he wore a peaked helmet and a gilded mail hauberk and held across his knees a jeweled-hilted scimitar. It seemed to Cormac that these men argued some matter just before setting out on some raid, as they were all fully armed. But he wasted no time on speculation. He tore the hangings aside with a mailed hand and strode into the room.

Amazement held the warriors frozen for an instant, and in that instant the giant Frank reached Kosru Malik's side.

The Turk, his dark features paling, sprang to his feet like a steel spring released, raising his scimitar, but even as he did so, Cormac braced his feet and smote with all his power. The Norse sword shivered the curved blade and, rending the gilded mail, severed the Turk's shoulder-bone and cleft his breast.

Cormac wrenched the heavy blade free from the split breastbone and with one foot on Kosru Malik's body, faced his foes like a lion at bay. His helmeted head was lowered, his cold blue eyes flaming from under the heavy black brows, and his mighty right hand held ready the stained sword. Nureddin had leaped to his feet and stood trembling in rage and astonishment. This sudden apparition came as near to unmanning him as anything had ever done. His thin, hawk-like features lowered in a wrathful snarl, his beard bristled and with a quick motion he unsheathed his ivory-hilted saber. Then even as he stepped forward and his warriors surged in behind him, a startling interruption occurred.

Cormac, a fierce joy surging in him as he braced himself for the charge, saw, on the other side of the great room, a wide door swing open and a host of armed warriors appear, accompanied by sundry of Nureddin's men, who wore empty scabbards and uneasy faces.

The Arab and his warriors whirled to face the newcomers. These men, Cormac saw, were dusty as if from long riding, and his memory flashed to the horsemen he had seen riding into the hills at dusk. Before them strode a tall, slender man, whose fine face was traced with lines of weariness, but whose aspect was that of a ruler of men. His garb was simple in comparison with the resplendent armor and silken attendants. And Cormac swore in amazed recognition.

Yet his surprize was no greater than that of the men of El Ghor.

"What do you in my castle, unannounced?" gasped Nureddin.

A giant in silvered mail raised his hand warningly and spoke sonorously: "The Lion of Islam, Protector of the Faithful, Yussef Ibn Eyyub, Salah-ud-din, Sultan of Sultans, needs no announcement to enter yours or any castle, Arab."

Nureddin stood his ground, though his followers began salaaming madly; there was iron in this Arabian renegade.

"My lord," said he stoutly, "it is true I did not recognize you when you first came into the chamber; but El Ghor is mine, not by virtue of right or aid or grant from any sultan, but the might of my own arm. Therefore, I make you welcome but do not beg your mercy for my hasty words."

Saladin merely smiled in a weary way. Half a century of intrigue and warring rested heavily on his shoulders. His brown eyes, strangely mild for so great a lord, rested on the silent Frankish giant who still stood with his mail-clad foot on what had been the chief Kosru Malik.

"And what is this?" asked the Sultan.

Nureddin scowled: "A Nazarene outlaw has stolen into my keep and assassinated my comrade, the Seljuk. I beg your leave to dispose of him. I will give you his skull, set in silver--"

A gesture stopped him. Saladin stepped past his men and confronted the dark, brooding warrior.

"I thought I had recognized those shoulders and that dark face," said the Sultan with a smile. "So you have turned your face east again, Lord Cormac?"

"Enough!" The deep voice of the Norman-Irish giant filled the chamber. "You have me in your trap; my life is forfeit. Waste not your time in taunts; send your jackals against me and make an end of it. I swear by my clan, many of them shall bite the dust before I die, and the dead will be more than the living!"

Nureddin's tall frame shook with passion; he gripped his hilt until the knuckles showed white. "Is this to be borne, my Lord?" he exclaimed fiercely. "Shall this Nazarene dog fling dirt into our faces--"

Saladin shook his head slowly, smiling as if at some secret jest: "It may be his is no idle boast. At Acre, at Azotus, at Joppa I have seen the skull on his shield glitter like a star of death in the mist, and the Faithful fall before his sword like garnered grain."

The great Kurd turned his head, leisurely surveying the ranks of silent warriors and the bewildered chieftains who avoided his level gaze.

"A notable concourse of chiefs, for these times of truce," he murmured, half to himself. "Would you ride forth in the night with all these warriors to fight genii in the desert, or to honor some ghostly sultan, Nureddin? Nay, nay, Nureddin, thou hast tasted the cup of ambition, meseemeth--and thy life is forfeit!"

The unexpectedness of the accusation staggered Nureddin, and while he groped for reply, Saladin followed it up: "It comes to me that you have plotted against me-- aye, that it was your purpose to seduce various Moslem and Frankish lords from their allegiances, and set up a kingdom of your own. And for that reason you broke the truce and murdered a good knight, albeit a Caphar, and burned his castle. I have spies, Nureddin."

The tall Arab glanced quickly about, as if ready to dispute the question with Saladin himself. But when he noted the number of the Kurd's warriors, and saw his own fierce ruffians shrinking away from him, awed, a smile of bitter contempt crossed his hawk-like features, and sheathing his blade, he folded his arms.

"God gives," he said simply, with the fatalism of the Orient.

Saladin nodded in appreciation, but motioned back a chief who stepped forward to bind the sheik. "Here is one," said the Sultan, "to whom you owe a greater debt than to me, Nureddin. I have heard Cormac FitzGeoffrey was brother-at-arms to the Sieur Gerard. You owe many debts of blood, oh Nureddin; pay one, therefore, by facing the lord Cormac with the sword."

The Arab's eyes gleamed suddenly. "And if I slay him-- shall I go free?"

"Who am I to judge?" asked Saladin. "It shall be as Allah wills it. But if you fight the Frank you will die, Nureddin, even though you slay him; he comes of a breed that slays even in their death-throes. Yet it is better to die by the sword than by the cord, Nureddin."

The sheik's answer was to draw his ivory-hilted saber. Blue sparks flickered in Cormac's eyes and he rumbled deeply like a wounded lion. He hated Saladin as he hated all his race, with the savage and relentless hatred of the Norman-Celt. He had ascribed the Kurd's courtesy to King Richard and the Crusaders to Oriental subtlety, refusing to believe that there could be ought but trickery and craftiness in a Saracen's mind. Now he saw in the Sultan's suggestion but the scheming of a crafty trickster to match two of his foes against each other, and a feline-like gloating over his victims. Cormac grinned without mirth. He asked no more from life than to have his enemy at sword-points. But he felt no gratitude toward Saladin, only a smoldering hate.

The Sultan and the warriors gave back, leaving the rivals a clear space in the center of the great room. Nureddin came forward swiftly, having donned a plain round steel cap with a mail drop that fell about his shoulders.

"Death to you, Nazarene!" he yelled, and sprang in with the pantherish leap and headlong recklessness of an Arab's attack. Cormac had no shield. He parried the hacking saber with upflung blade, and slashed back. Nureddin caught the heavy blade on his round buckler, which he turned slightly slantwise at the instant of impact, so that the stroke glanced off. He returned the blow with a thrust that rasped against Cormac's coif, and leaped a spear's length backward to avoid the whistling sweep of the Norse sword.

Again he leaped in, slashing, and Cormac caught the saber on his left forearm. Mail links parted beneath the keen edge, and blood spattered, but almost simultaneously the Norse sword crashed under the Arab's arm, bones cracked and Nureddin was flung his full length to the floor. Warriors gasped as they realized the full power of the Irishman's tigerish strokes.

Nureddin's rise from the floor was so quick that he almost seemed to rebound from his fall. To the onlookers it seemed that he was not hurt, but the Arab knew. His mail had held; the sword edge had not gashed his flesh, but the impact of that terrible blow had snapped a rib like a rotten twig, and the realization that he could not long avoid the Frank's rushes filled him with a wild beast determination to take his foe with him to Eternity.

Cormac was looming over Nureddin, sword high, but the Arab nerving himself to a dynamic burst of superhuman quickness, sprang up as a cobra leaps from its coil, and struck with desperate power. Full on Cormac's bent head the whistling saber clashed, and the Frank staggered as the keen edge bit through steel cap and coif links into his scalp. Blood jetted down his face, but he braced his feet and struck back with all the power of arm and shoulders behind the sword. Again Nureddin's buckler blocked the stroke, but this time the Arab had no time to turn the shield, and the heavy blade struck squarely. Nureddin went to his knees beneath the stroke, bearded face twisted in agony. With tenacious courage he reeled up again, shaking the shattered buckler from his numbed and broken arm, but even as he lifted the saber, the Norse sword crashed down, cleaving the Moslem helmet and splitting the skull to the teeth.

Cormac set a foot on his fallen foe and wrenched free his gory sword. His fierce eyes met the whimsical gaze of Saladin.

"Well, Saracen," said the Irish warrior challengingly, "I have killed your rebel for you."

"And your enemy," reminded Saladin.

"Aye," Cormac grinned bleakly and ferociously. "I thank you--though well I know it was no love of me or mine that prompted you to send the Arab against me. Well--make an end, Saracen."

"Why do you hate me, Lord Cormac?" asked the Sultan curiously.

Cormac snarled. "Why do I hate any of my foes? You are no more and no less than any other robber chief, to me. You tricked Richard and the rest with courtly words and fine deeds, but you never deceived me, who well knew you sought to win by deceit where you could not gain by force of arms."

Saladin shook his head, murmuring to himself. Cormac glared at him, tensing himself for a sudden leap that would carry the Kurd with him into the Dark. The Norman-Gael was a product of his age and his country; among the warring chiefs of blood-drenched Ireland, mercy was unknown and chivalry an outworn and forgotten myth. Kindness to a foe was a mark of weakness; courtesy to an enemy a form of craft, a preparation for treachery; to such teachings had Cormac grown up, in a land where a man took every advantage, gave no quarter and fought like a blood-mad devil if he expected to survive.

Now at a gesture from Saladin, those crowding the door gave back.

"Your way is open, Lord Cormac."

The Gael glared, his eyes narrowing to slits: "What game is this?" he growled. "Shall I turn my back to your blades? Out on it!"

"All swords are in their sheaths," answered the Kurd. "None shall harm you."

Cormac's lion-like head swung from side to side as he glared at the Moslems.

"You honestly mean I am to go free, after breaking the truce and slaying your jackals?"

"The truce was already broken," answered Saladin. "I find in you no fault. You have repaid blood for blood, and kept your faith to the dead. You are rough and savage, but I would fain have men like you in mine own train. There is a fierce loyalty in you, and for this I honor you."

Cormac sheathed his sword ungraciously. A grudging admiration for this weary-faced Moslem was born in him and it angered him. Dimly he realized at last that this attitude of fairness, justice and kindliness, even to foes, was not a crafty pose of Saladin's, not a manner of guile, but a natural nobility of the Kurd's nature. He saw suddenly embodied in the Sultan, the ideals of chivalry and high honor so much talked of--and so little practiced--by the Frankish knights. Blondel had been right then, and Sieur Gerard, when they argued with Cormac that high-minded chivalry was no mere romantic dream of an outworn age, but had existed, and still existed and lived in the hearts of certain men. But Cormac was born and bred in a savage land where men lived the desperate existence of the wolves whose hides covered their nakedness. He suddenly realized his own innate barbarism and was ashamed. He shrugged his lion's shoulders.

"I have misjudged you, Moslem," he growled. "There is fairness in you."

"I thank you, Lord Cormac," smiled Saladin. "Your road to the west is clear."

And the Moslem warriors courteously salaamed as Cormac FitzGeoffrey strode from the royal presence of the slender noble who was Protector of the Califs, Lion of Islam, Sultan of Sultans.